A HOUSE FOR EVERYONE

by Betty Miles
illustrated by Jo Lowrey

pinwheel books
knopf/pantheon

FIRST PINWHEEL BOOKS EDITION—MARCH, 1973. Originally published by Alfred A. Knopf, Inc. in 1958. Copyright © 1958 by Betty Miles and Jo Lowrey. All rights reserved under International and Pan-American Copyright Conventions. Published in the United States by Random House, Inc., and simultaneously in Toronto, Canada, by Random House of Canada, Limited, Toronto. Manufactured in the United States of America. *Library of Congress Catalog Card Number:* 72-9558. ISBN: 0-394-82618-3.

Everybody has a house

to come inside of.

A house
is for
eating
and sleeping,
for taking
a bath
and hanging
up clothes.

A house is for having fun
with other people.

Some houses are old,

and some are new.

Some
are in
the city,
and reach
up high.

Some are in the country,

and stretch sideways.

Every house has somebody
to come inside it
and say, "I'm hungry,
is it time for supper?"

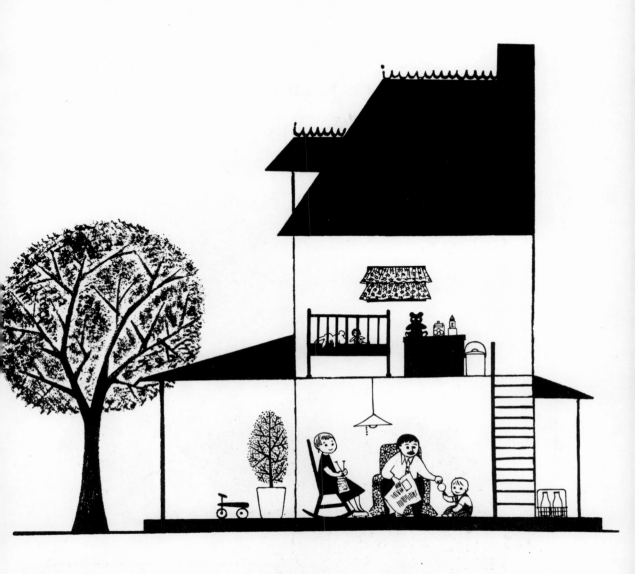

People live together in houses
in different ways.
This house has a mother and father
and a baby in it.

This house has a grandmother,
a mother, and two children.

In this house

      lives an old gentleman

with his five cats.

Here is a house with two aunts
and some plants.

And here is a house where twelve people
live and work together.

In the daytime, people go

away from their houses.

They go to school,

or to the store,

or to work outside,

or inside.

But they come home again
to play,

and to work,

to sing, and to make funny jokes,
or just to be together.

The house is where they belong.
It is what they come back to.

After supper,

      lights are on in all the houses.

Children begin to go to bed.

The children are tucked
warm and soft in their beds.

Everywhere, the children are asleep,

in all the houses.

goodnight